revolvinghammer

ed.
kristen bevilacqua
and
scott o. brown

cyberosia publishing
somerville, massachusetts

REVOLVING HAMMER
ISBN 0-9709474-4-5

Cyberosia Publishing, LLC
8 Richardson Terrace
Somerville, MA 02145-2536
www.cyberosia.com

For Cyberosia:
Scott O. Brown, Publisher
Kristen Bevilacqua, Co-publisher

First edition, April 2002
10 9 8 7 6 5 4 3 2 1

Cover Illustration and Design: Elizabeth Mitchell
Book Design: Scott O. Brown

Printed by Brenner Printing.

table of contents

written by: brad collins

artwork and lettering by: jason badower

career suspect

DATE NIGHT written by Marc Bryant drawn by Mal Jones

BLAMBOT CUSTOM LETTERING FONT FROM WWW.PIEKOSARTS.COM

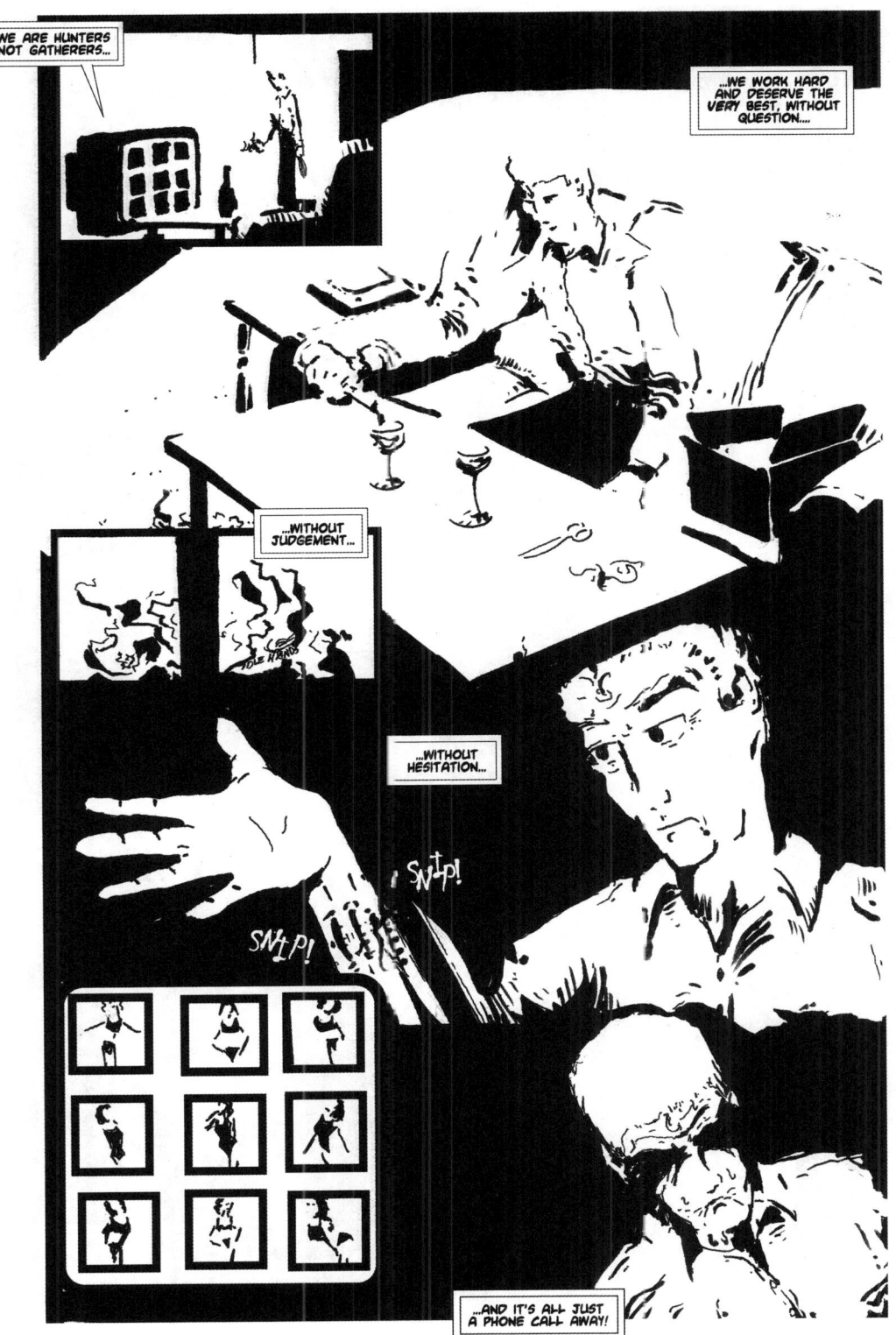

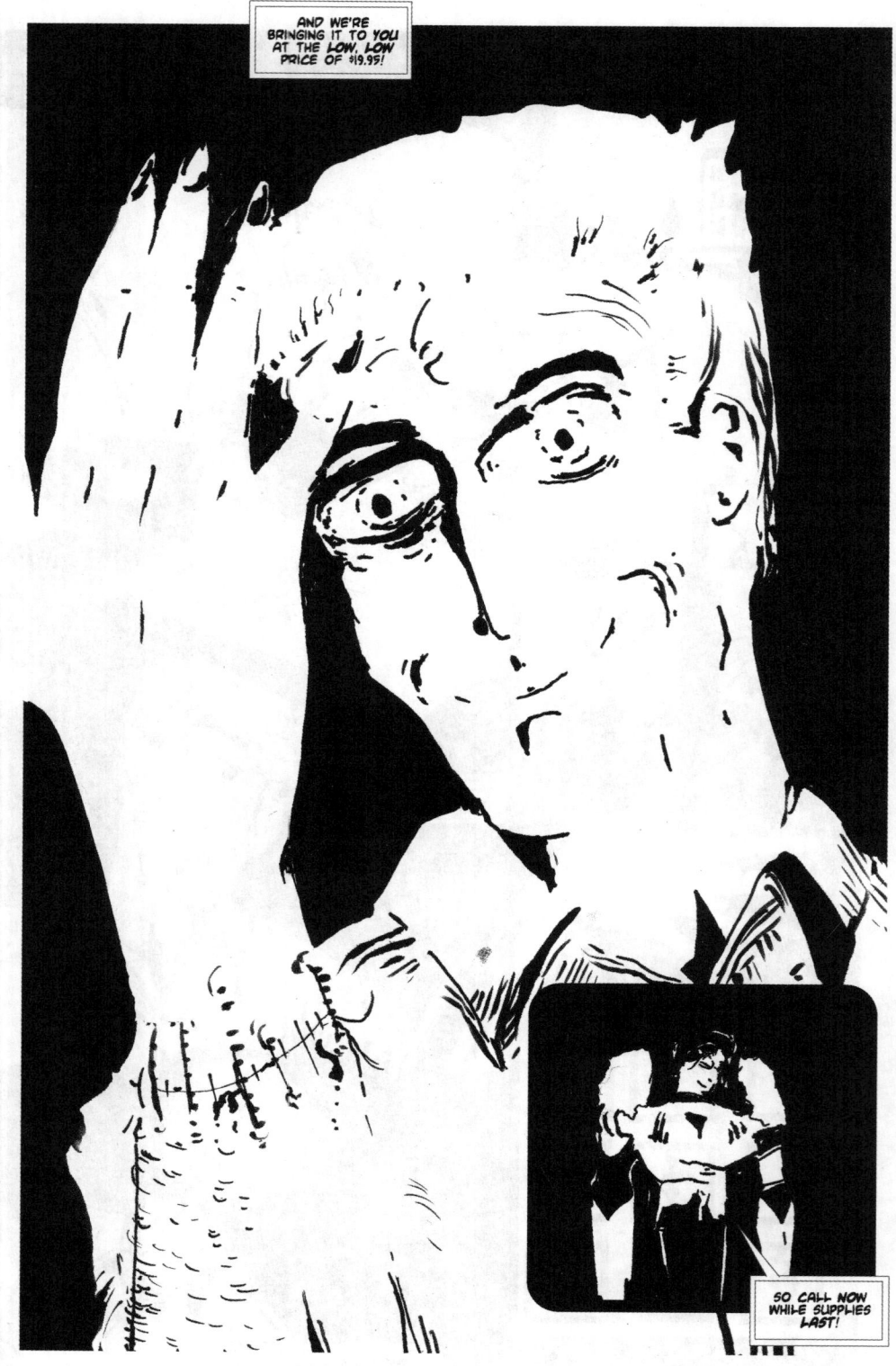

END DATE NIGHT

SEX USED TO BE SO EASY...

ALL YOU NEEDED WERE TWO WILLING PEOPLE. A SMALL CHEMICAL REACTION. AND YOU COULD PRETTY MUCH LET INSTINCT TAKE OVER.

THE ONLY PROPS YOU NEEDED WERE MAYBE SOME PRESS-ON FINGERNAILS AND MINT "ALTOIDS".

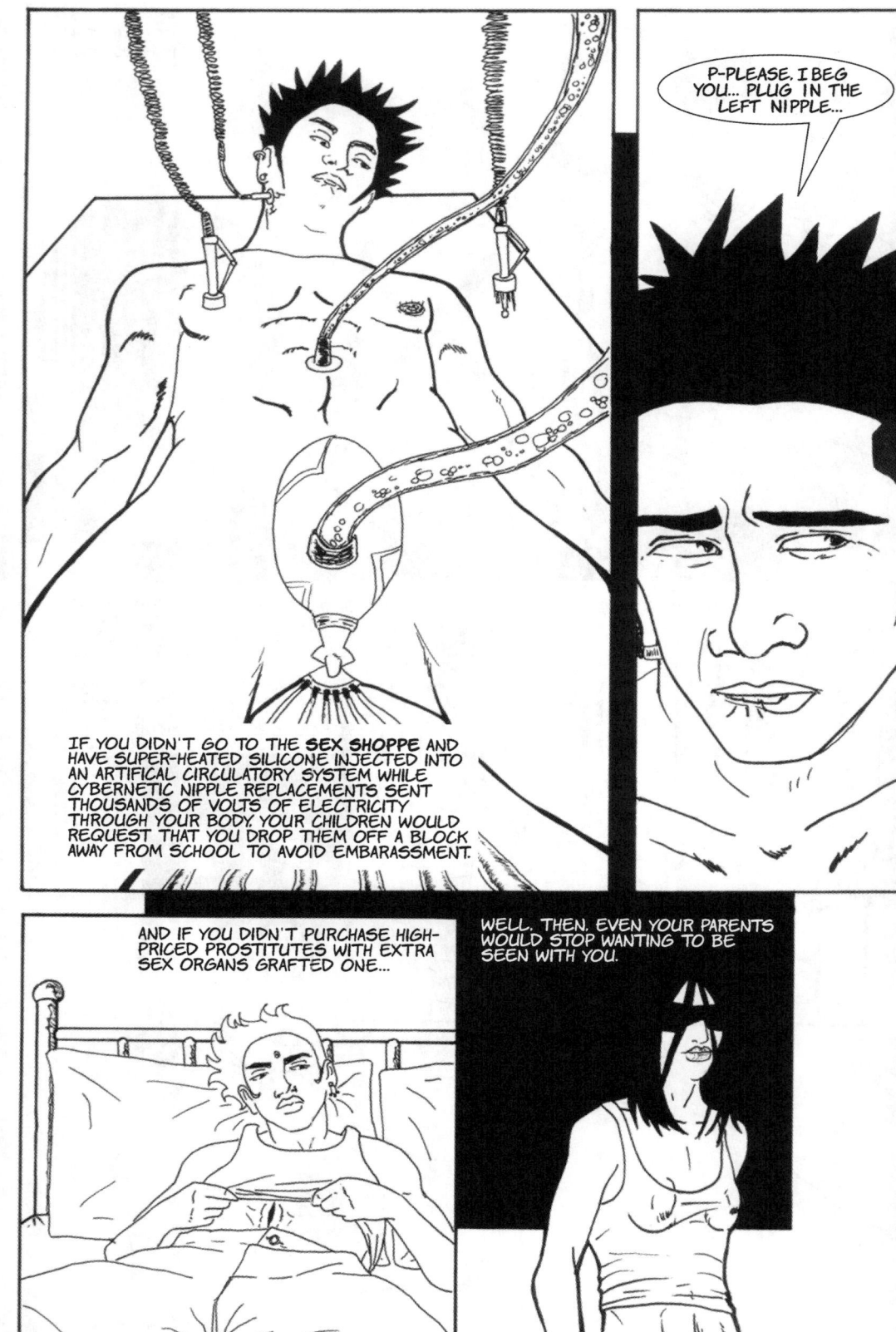

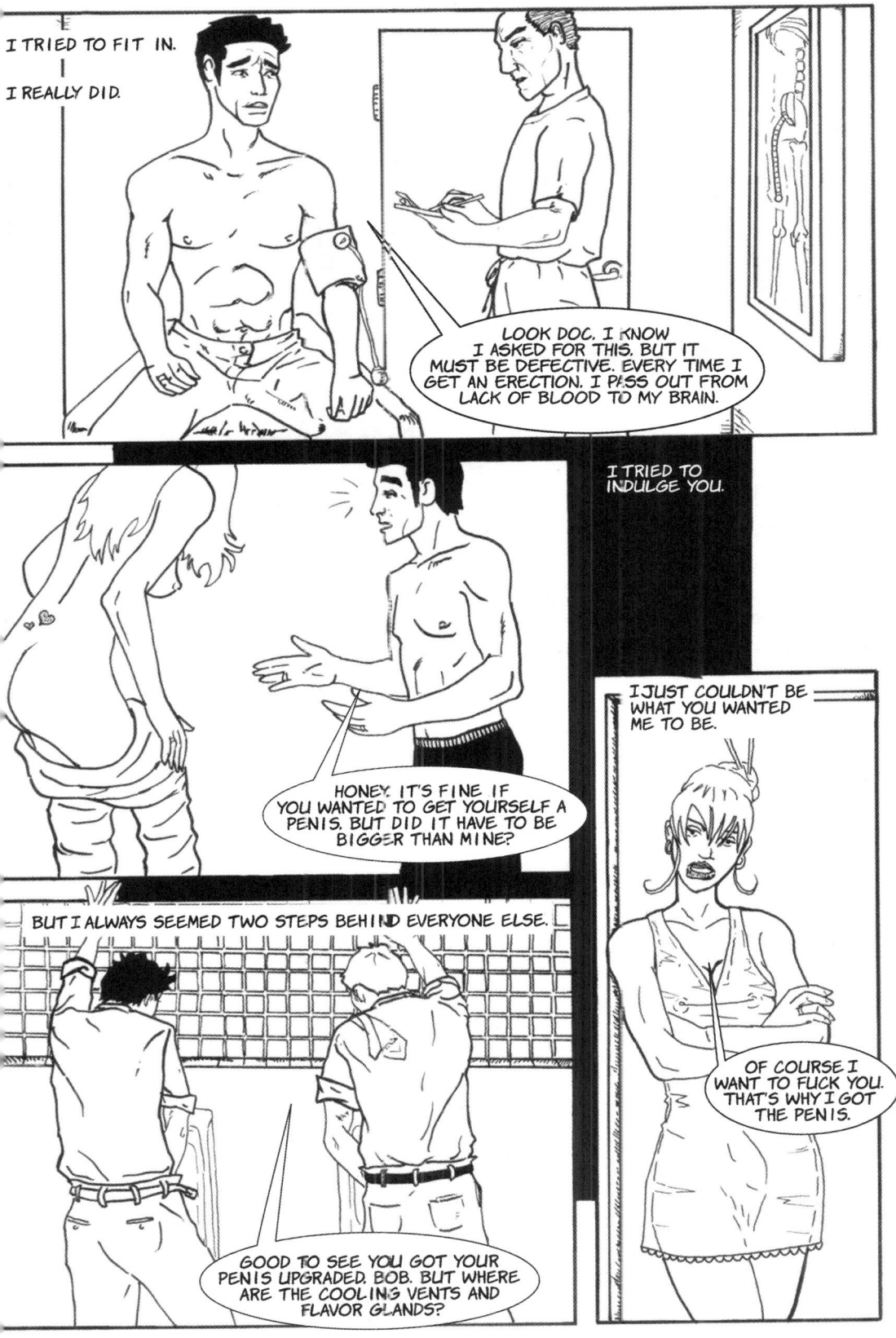

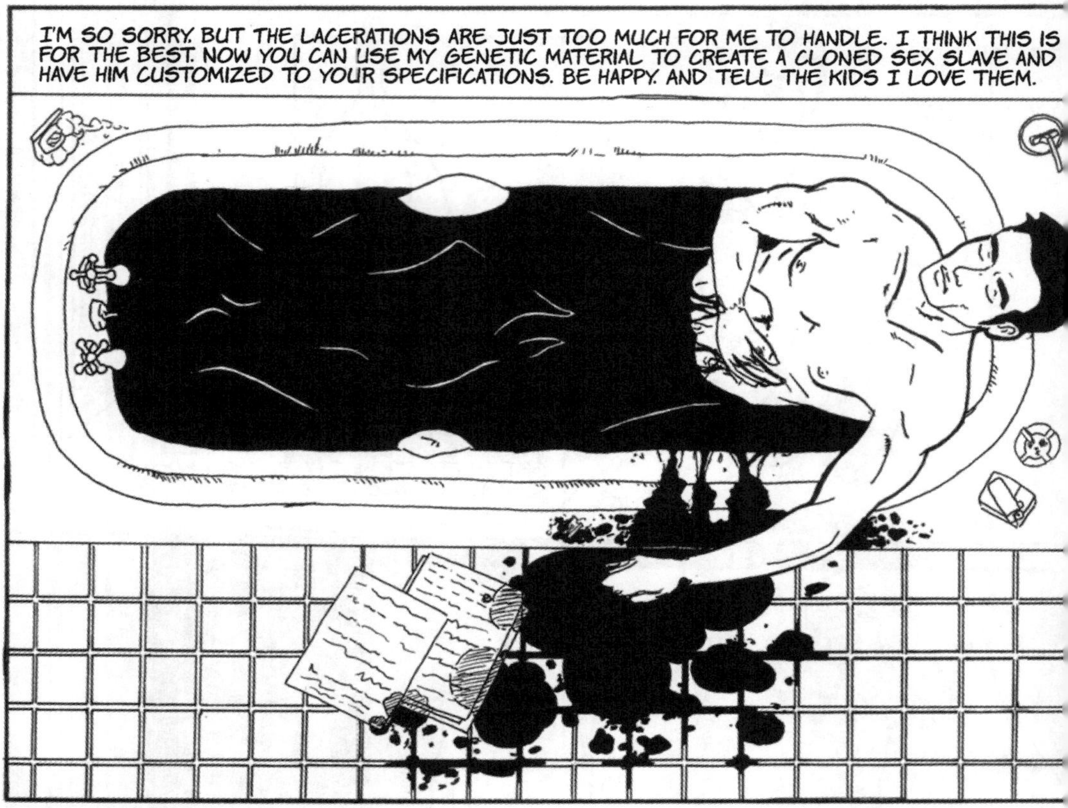

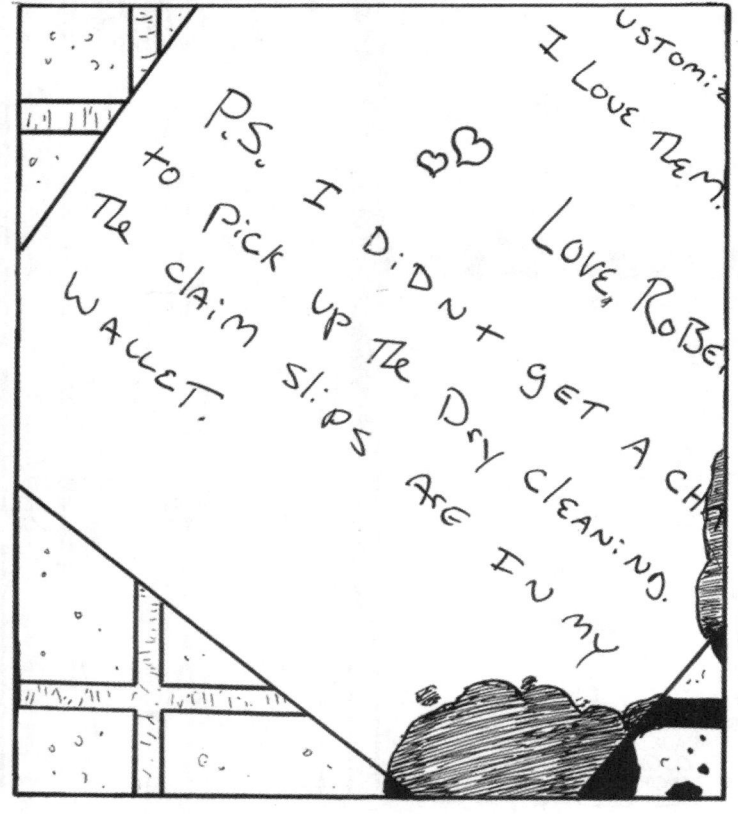

Words - Alistair Pulling
Pictures - Bevis Musson

"To Whom It May Concern..."
words - Andrew Foley
art - W. Strang-Frost

Back in college, I had a teacher who liked to say "that which is possible replaces that which is not."

CROWN & PIGLET

OPEN

He was right; there is something in the wiring of the human mind that allows most to accept their circumstances.

For a long time, I've obeyed my programming. But not tonight. Tonight that which is does not replace that which is impossible.

OPEN

This was a long time in coming. Too long a time, really, but it's never too late to make things right.

Right?

Right.

Once the Crown and Piglet was more than just a bar. It was always more than a bar, to me at least.

It's hard to describe just what it was, the role it played in my life. I don't have a wife, barely have a girlfriend, never had many I'd consider close friends... But I always had a place; that was enough for me.

I wasn't the only one who felt that way. There were others. The C and P was as much a home to some as the places they rented, the bachelor suites with the guy upstairs with the crappy music and the roaches in the kitchen.

We used to get things done, there. Good things.

When a waitress' apartment burnt down, we held a special night for her. By the time all the money was counted, she had more than she knew what to do with. She got the basics taken care of, then gave the rest to Rod.

The C and P was the closest thing Rod had to a home. If he wasn't here, he was lying on a bench, or under it, waiting for the doors to open. As often as I had to toss him out the doors, I fed him, gave him shelter. Sometimes somebody would sneak him a beer, which bothered me—Rod obviously had problems, and I didn't want to make them worse.

I could never stay mad at whoever weakened to Rod's pleas. They were just trying to do right by a member of the community.

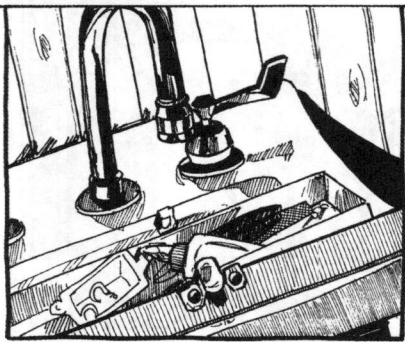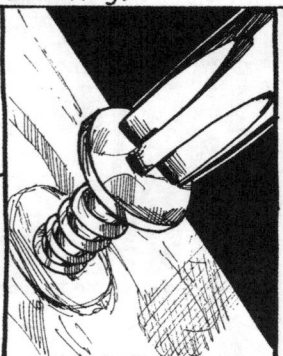

It's the sense of community that's missing now; somehow it's been lost.

Somehow—like I don't know how it happened. It's no mystery—I got older, the world became less black and white. I compromised when I should have fought for what I deep down knew was right.

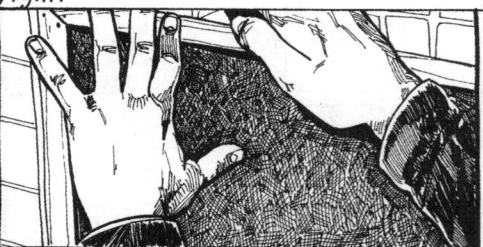

The compromises got easier and easier to make; the rationalizations seemed more feasible. And then, seemingly overnight, everything had changed.

It was only after Rod died that I was able to appreciate the communal aspect of the bar. There was a pall over the place for weeks. That homeless drunk had more friends than he ever realized.

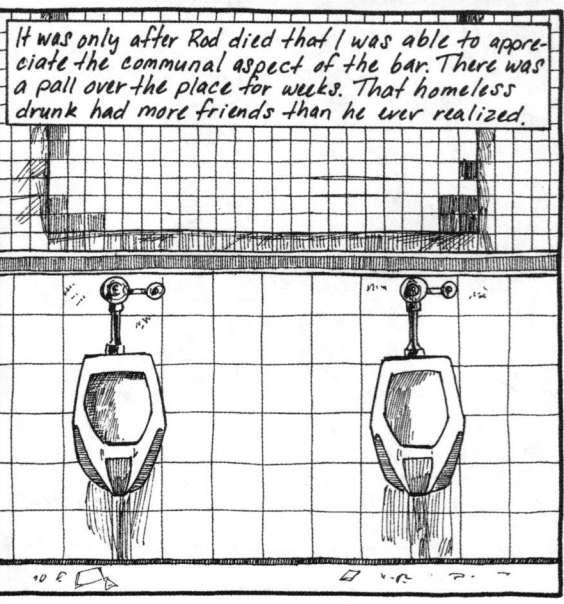

I don't know who carved his name into the men's room chalk board, but it seemed an eminently suitable memorial. When George was killed by a drunk driver, his name ended up on the board, too. These people would not be forgotten, not as long as the bar was here.

Over the years, the list on the board grew.

A couple of years ago the name 'Lindsay' appeared there, beneath the others.

I don't think I've ever known a Lindsay.

But someone did and they carved his name on the board beneath Rod's and George's, Maxie's and Wain's. I'd known people were coming to my bar that I didn't know, people for whom it was an integral part of their lives, as it had once been part of mine. And now one of them had died, and the tradition of the place was carried on. That was enough for me.

The place would survive without my being there every night. I never left, not completely, but from that point on I came to my bar less and less. And every time I did, I found that it was less and less than the place it had been.

So be it, I thought. The place was more popular than ever, brought in more money than I'll ever be able to spend. Someday it would die on its own; until then I was satisfied to leave it be. At least I thought I was.

Until Thursday.

The day Rod's name appeared on the men's room chalk board was the day I realized I was part of something more than a business, that the Crown and Piglet was something vital and alive. The day his name disappeared was the day I knew all that was lost forever.

Someone had eradicated his name, carved it from existence, tried to erase Rod from existence. And if his name could be treated so shabbily, it would only be a matter of time before someone did the same to George, or Lindsay, or the others.

This morning I got up, and looked in the mirror, and didn't recognize the person looking back at me.

So, no more compromises... That which is possible is no longer an acceptable substitute for that which isn't.

I don't know who scratched Rod's name off the board, but they will never again sit at my table, never find solace or comfort in my bar. They won't be allowed to vandalize and destroy the memory of what the C and P used to be.

Not anymore.

I've done what I've done because what's possible would someday overwhelm what wasn't. This was the only way to keep the good times from being contaminated by the bad, the only way to preserve the ideal.

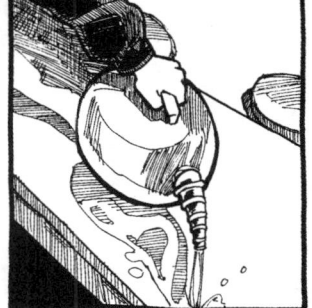

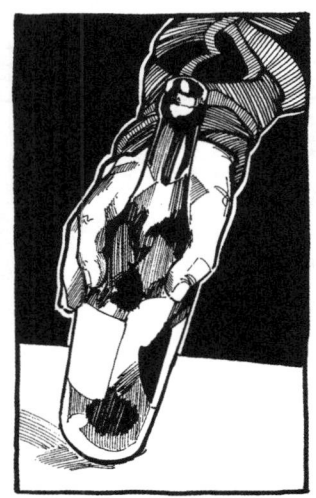

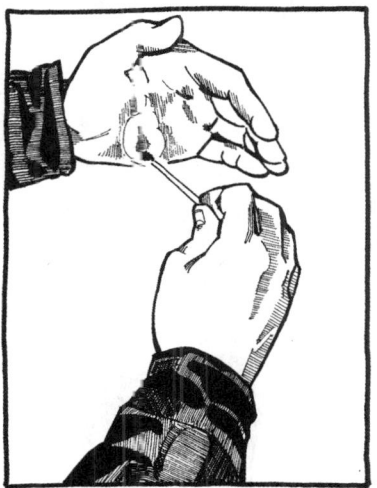

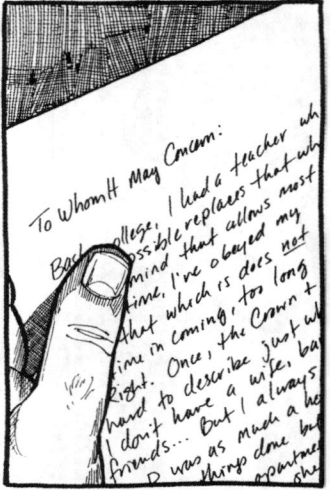

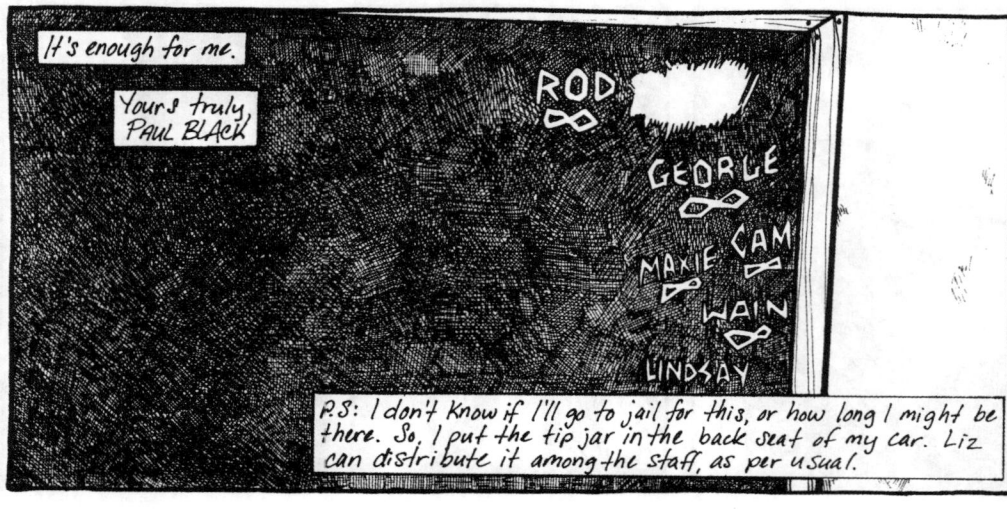

since 1986,
our pledge of
the highest quality
exotic novelties and
toys is still goes.

-BORN FOR PORN!!

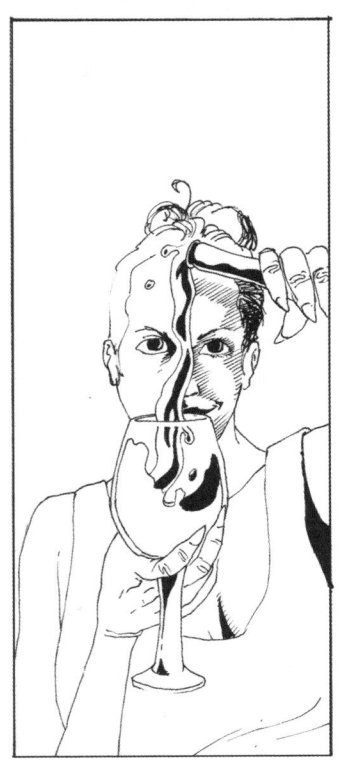

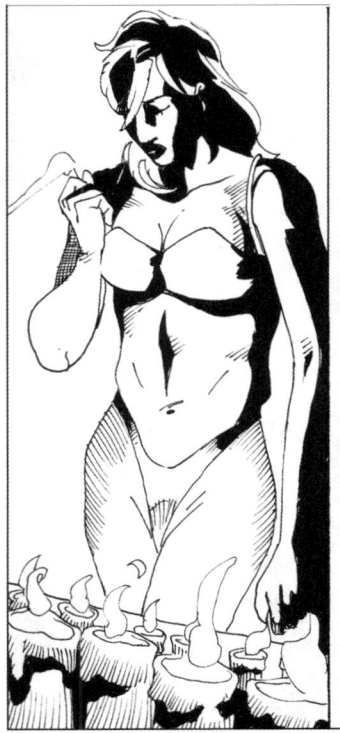

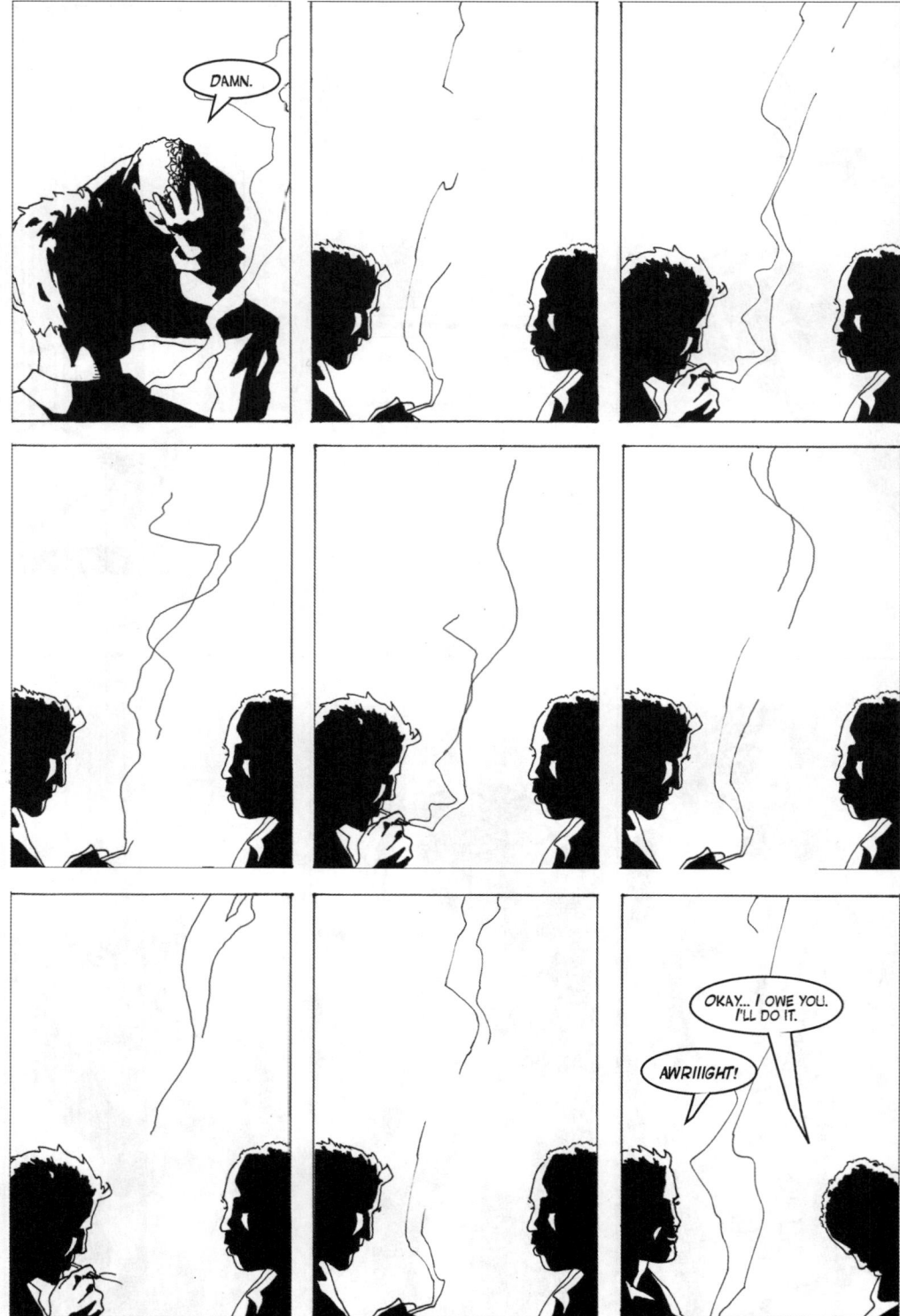

THANKS, MAN. REALLY. YOU CAN'T POSSIBLY KNOW HOW MUCH THIS MEANS TO ME.

THAT'S WHAT FRIENDS ARE FOR, I GUESS.

SAY, MAN, YOU SURE SHE'S HOME?

YEAH, I HEARD HER CLUNKIN' AROUND UP HERE WHEN WE WERE TALKIN'.

ALMOST THERE. YOU READY TO DO THIS?

(sigh) AS I'LL EVER BE.

HI, HUNNNEEEEEE...

...HELLO, XAVIER

HONEY?

JESUS CHRIST! SHE'S OUT COLD! I DON'T THINK SHE'S BREATHING...

I DON'T FELL ANY PULSE! OH, HOLD ON, BABY. I PRAY TO GOD YOU DIDN'T DRINK THIS WHOLE BOTTLE!

XAVIER, YOU GOTTA HELP! I THINK SHE'S GOT ALOCOHOL POISONING. CALL 911 OR SOMETHING. SHE'S NOT BREATHING!

OHMIGOD, BABY, WHAT'D YOU DO?! WHAT'D YOU DO?! WE GOTTA DO SOMETHING, XAVIER! WHY AREN'T YOU BREATHING, BABY? SHITSHITSHITSHITSHIT!

CAL'S TRICK

IT WAS THE KIND OF DAY THAT OPPRESSED YOU, THE KIND THAT BEAT YOU DOWN AND LEFT YOU HOPELESS, WITHERED INSIDE.

AND THEN CAL ARRIVED.

EVERYONE WHO HUNG AT THE SHIP KNEW CAL. ANYONE WHO HUNG AT ANY BAR IN THE DOWN-TOWN CORE KNEW THIS CRAZY OLD MAN, THIS URBAN GYPSY.

HE WAS A FIGURE OF MYTHICAL PROPORTIONS, A TRICK-STER WHO COULD APPEAR AT ANY MOMENT AND TURN THE EVERYDAY SURREAL LIKE VINEGAR CURDLING MILK.

PAGE ONE

PAGE EIGHT

AUNTY

words: Walter Conley
pictures: Becky Cloonan

Exhibit-A

Story by Scott O. Brown, Illustrations by Andrew Foley

I'm standing at the intersection of US Highways 39 and 251 in the dead center of nowhere in the mountains of Alabama. The Wal-Mart is behind me. I'm facing a Texaco gas station full of rust-gnawed pick-ups older than I am. This intersection is the only one with a traffic light for three miles. Everyone here is an Olin or a Leighanne or a Billyjoebob. Everyone drives through this intersection; it's the only way to get anywhere. The interstate is ten miles south and the trailer park is four the

opposite. And unless you have a car, there's no way to get out here.

It's November, and I'm sweating in this overcoat. I don't understand why th aren't any seasons here. Actually, there are two, summer and winter, but nothing in between. It isn't natural.

I feel my hair stick to the back of my neck and notice for the first time that i smells like body. It doesn't stink. It just smells like a human body—oily and salty an just a little dirty. The light changes. I walk to the middle of the street and glance at t oncoming traffic. Only three cars. They aren't worth the effort. If I'm going to do th right, I need at least a good dozen. That could take all day.

A slight breeze whips around me and I catch a whiff of gasoline fumes. Fron the under the kiosk at the Texaco, I hear someone say something horribly incompre- hensible in one of the worst, sludgy, ignorant accents I've heard in hours. And then hear

a woman answer, "Okay, honey." I try to get a look at who's talking. A guy with cig rettes rolled up in the sleeve of his t-shirt and a life-sized, caked-up barbie with too much make-up and hair five inches tall. The scene is too gross, and I turn my attenti back to the task at hand. But I glance back anyway. I hope they never have children.

The light turns again. No cars at all. Rush hour should kick in any time. The pavement is hot on my bare feet. I peel the hair off the back of my neck and sit for a minute. Once traffic gets a good roar, I'll have all the rusted-out pick-ups and fifth- hand SUVs I could ask for.

Tires screech to my left and I turn just in time to see a Dodge pick-up get folded up in half beneath an eighteen-wheeler. It's a good quarter mile down. I light another cigarette. A bunch of cars pull over to help. Someone hollers into a cell pho

I'm torn for a second, but rush hour won't really kick in for another fifteen minutes so I stroll over to the accident, pulling my coat tighter against the warm breeze. Nothing's on fire but the sun as it dips halfway below the tree line. They mill about, bumping into one another and barking orders like they're important, like their power will be gone at any moment. It's a moment that's rapidly approaching as I hea a cacophony of sirens roaring closer. Everyone looks okay. Battered, but not dead. I half-heartedly ask someone if I can help but get shoved to the side. My coat comes open a little at the top, and I can feel the last beams of sunlight hit my bare chest.

I jaunt across the street, taking advantage of the accident-congested traffic. There's a good row of cars backed up. The hill dips down a quarter mile back, and th

ıggish accumulation of cars disap-
ars at the decline. The light turns
d. Everyone who thought they could
n the yellow is stuck in the intersec-
n, backing everyone up from all
ints. I stand in the middle. I can feel
e veins in my arms as the blood
rges through my body. Time to give
ese rotten fuckers a glorious ray of
nshine.

I pull my coat open and ex-
se myself. Someone honks.

The ride to the station is uneventful aside from being called a pervert. If
ey want a real pervert, they should check out the nightlife in Chicago some time.
y coat's come open, and I can't cover myself back up. The cops don't notice. I'm
ried in the back seat, and they don't even look in the rearview mirror when talking
me.

I find the fact that the police station is in the same shopping center as Wal-
art to be one of the highpoints of this small town. It's not a separate building. It's
e last two storefronts on the far end of the plaza next door to a Chinese restaurant.
ley park all the squad cars around back. I can't even begin to count the number of
nes I've drunk myself to nothing behind the Wal-Mart with the police station only
ty yards away. That's the one redeeming part of living in the middle of Nowhere,
labama in a town of a single traffic light. You can buy liquor in grocery stores.

After calling my mother, I sit in my cell alone. I'm not by myself. The local
unk, Reginald, is passed out face first on the floor, smelling like dried puke and
dy odor. I may as well consider the cell mine. The officers bought a pair of jeans
d a T-shirt for me. Either they were stunned by my manhood or too embarrassed
see someone of the same sex naked. Or maybe they were just afraid. I can stand
ked in the shower, naked in my home, naked in the swimming hole, but I can't be
ked in front of other people.

The clock says eight o'clock. My mom should be getting off work by now,
aking a beeline for the precinct to gnaw my throat out. I know my Dad won't
ow. A car could've hit me, and he would've complained about having to go to the
neral. Mom will go ballistic. I'm not worried. If she tries anything smart, dad will
st have to bail her out, too. Just like last time.

The clock says nine o'clock, and no
one's shown up. The officer offered me
coffee and tried to talk to me all friendly-
like about fishing with my dad. I know the
tricks. I'm smarter, faster, and better
looking. And I'd lock even better if I
weren't wearing these stupid clothes, so I
take them off while he's babbling about
trout. He stops mid-sentence and says
something he'd think was pithy. He turns

his back to me, and I start swinging it in a circle. "Yo, dumbass," I call out, "Can you do this with yours, or do you just jerk off all day long?"

The clock says ten o'clock and no one's here yet. The shift changed. I decided not to put my clothes back on. Reginald woke up and passed out again. I'm getting bored. It's never taken them this long to bail me out before. But that's okay. I can play the waiting game. It's not like they can leave me here, is it? The clock says eleven o'clock, and I put my clothes back on to get some sleep. No point in tempting poor brain-dead Reginald with my naked ass.

The clock says twelve o'clock and I can't sleep. The first time it barely took them fifteen minutes to get here. I've been here six hours. I think the record was forty minutes, and that's only because my little brother was stuck at band rehearsal. I hope they're okay.

The clock says three o'clock. I guess I dozed. My idiot parents, the ones who took me from one of the apices of civilization and brought me to this pisswater redneck convention, aren't here yet. Reginald's still gone. Looks like he puked in his sleep.

The clock says four o'clock. And I am aware as I drift off.

Burning sunrise light slips through the blinds across the room, waking me up. I'm the only one there. "Have my parents been here yet?"

"No."

"They call?" I rub my eyes.

"Said, let you stew."

Bastards. I stretch, yawn, eye the doughnuts on the desk across the room. I kick the bars and bang on the plaster coated concrete walls. I do this for five minutes before I stub my toe. It's not like I robbed a bank. I just wanted people to pay attention. I wanted them to stop and look. My parents never do. They avert their eyes to everything. Even me. All I did was flash those people. I had done nothing wrong. I didn't stop traffic or endanger lives. Traffic was already dead on the asphalt. There is nothing wrong with what I did.

An officer offers me doughnuts and mediocre coffee. My dad shows up about then. I set my coffee down on the ground and stand facing the bars. I make sure I'm out of arm's reach. My father stands the same distance on the opposite side. He's silent and staring. I don't say anything. He doesn't move. He doesn't even look like he's breathing. I shift my weight from foot to foot. He doesn't. I

push my oily hair back out of my eyes. He turns his head slightly to the right, keeping his eyes focussed on me. Then he leaves.

I take a quick, single step up to the bars and crane my neck to see him walking out the front.

"Dad, come back!" I holler. He doesn't respond. The door closes behind him.

An hour later the officers unlock my cell and let me go. There's nothing outside for me but an empty parking lot.

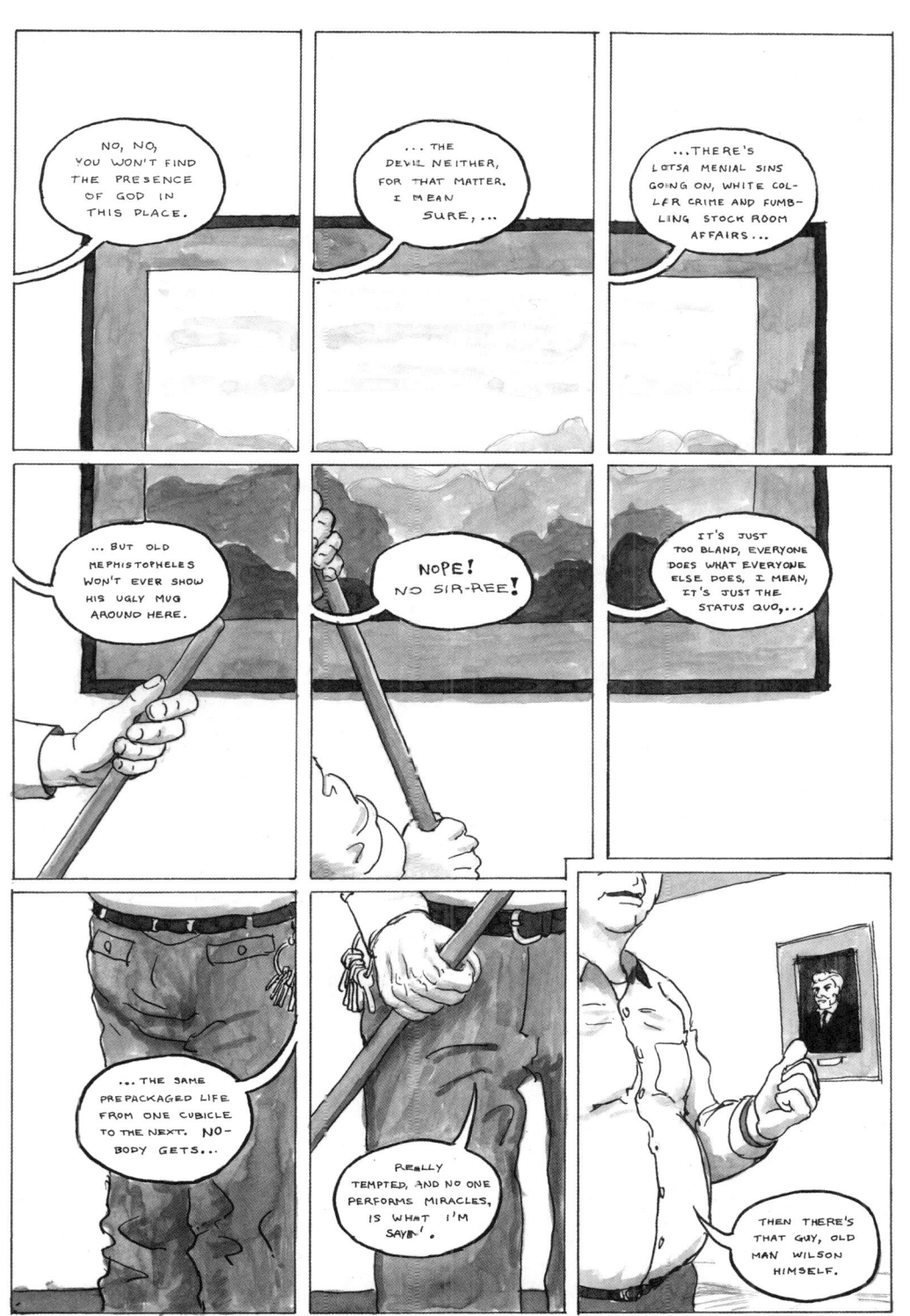